VILLAGE PenDelfin TALES

THE Family

First Published 1987
All rights reserved

Published by

PenDelfin Studios Limited,
Burnley, Lancashire, England

ISBN 1 870624 009
Printed in Great Britain by
Peter Scott (Printers) Limited,
Burnley, Lancashire, England

Foreword

These little books are designed for the entertainment of Collectors of PenDelfin. They are, like the models, for the young in heart.

Over the years, from many parts of the world, faithful friends of the Rabbit Family have bombarded the studios in England with requests for stories about their favourite characters . . . here they are at last.

With threat and with bribe, the PenDelfin designers have been persuaded to, temporarily, lay down their modelling tools and take up their pens – to produce a series of books featuring their own creations. They became so enchanted by the whole picture-book business that they invested in a camera and had a wonderful time, with sand and rocks and twigs and lengths of green velvet – conjuring up miniature table-top landscapes as settings for the Village.

Collectors may find some useful ideas in the illustrations, for their own 'display corners'.

3

The Old Hole Homestead

THE FAMILY

by

JEAN WALMSLEY HEAP

Models & Pictures
by
Jean Walmsley Heap
and
Doreen Noel Roberts

6

Contents

PenDelfin Village

The home of the Rabbit Family lies at the foot of old Pendle, the legendary witch-hill, in the wild and beautiful Northern part of England. Its charter dates from June the second, nineteen hundred and fifty-three, the day that Queen Elizabeth II was crowned.

The Family

Long Ago, in their green and giddy youth, Mother Rabbit married Father Rabbit and everybody in PenDelfin Village went to the wedding.

They had a wonderful time.

They all enjoyed the cakes and ale, the speeches and the presents, they even danced in the thunderstorm that flooded the village green. The thunder rolled, the lightning flashed, the drums and cymbals thumped and crashed – and only the oldest, most crotchety rabbit, was heard to grumble as he hopped off home: "It can't last, of course, it can't *last*!" Whether he meant the weather or the wedding – nobody bothered to ask . . .

Now, although Father Rabbit was handsome and brave – and although he loved his new wife very dearly, the whole village knew that he possessed 'neither carrot nor cabbage patch'.*
As a younger son, of excellent pedigree, he had inherited his fair share of the family estate – (Two Thousand Cabbage Seeds and a Hole in the Riverbank) – unfortunately, being far from thrifty and naturally generous, the cabbage seeds were long since spent and all that remained was the Hole.

Here, he took his bride.

It was a nice Hole, as holes go. It was large and dry and sandy, in the roots of a hollow tree. Pendle Water flowed past its door; Pendle Hill sheltered it from the northern winds; Pendle Forest provided fuel and food and good company. Mother Rabbit was enchanted.

"Who cares about cabbage?" she said, "Let us eat cake!" – and away she whirled to dust the sand off the table and unpack the wedding presents.

Father Rabbit, who firmly believes that all things are for the best in the best of all possible

* Cabbage seeds were very rare and precious and used as money in those days, most of the forest creatures lived on herbs and nettles.

worlds, was delighted to have such a practical little wife. "Now," he said, as he carried in the cooking stove, "here we shall live, quietly and simply and Happily Ever After!" And, for quite a time, they did.

The first baby rabbit was called Robert.* His parents were delighted. Then came the next – and the next – and as the Family grew, the Hole grew. Father Rabbit would take up his spade and dig out a few more rooms. It seemed a pleasant, sensible way to live and everybody was happy – until the arrival of UNCLE SOAMES.

Soames was smart. Soames was a Rabbit of Property. He always managed to make Father Rabbit feel like a very small rabbit indeed . . .

"You ought to be ashamed, little brother," said Soames, "living in a hole in the ground!"

"It's a nice hole!" said Father Rabbit, "most rabbits live in holes . . ."

"Not if they're smart!" said Uncle Soames, and off he zoomed down the river in his glossy new boat, to his suite at the Castle Tavern.

---

* Robert was last heard of in Florida, U.S.A. where, we understand, he is taming the natives.

ROSA PAINTED THIS PICTURE. *Rosa is the artistic friend of the Rabbit Family. She painted the picture for Mother Rabbit and it cheered her up no end. (After the very rude remarks of Uncle Soames, the whole Family wanted everybody to see that their Hole was no small, mean abode – but a very wonderful and exciting place to live.)*

Thumper is playing all Mother Rabbit's favourite tunes on the old Honky-tonk piano and awakening the babies who were sent to bed hours ago. His "backing group" includes Barney – who sings all the wrong tunes.

Rosa had to paint Uncle Soames' portrait from memory, because the wily old rascal was already on the high seas – back to his deals and diddles. (The hatchet in the tree root belongs to Barney, who had generously offered to cut his Uncle down to size . . .)

Father Rabbit is not in the picture because he had gone off to bed with a headache, a jug of nettle beer, and a large Map of the World.

Early the next morning, Father Rabbit gathered his Family together and solemnly addressed them:

"Dear Family," he said, "much as I love you, the time has come for us to part. Uncle Soames is possibly right – and I, alas, am probably wrong. A hole, even our own most excellent Hole, is not, after all, an ideal home . . ." Here, the Family noisily disagreed.

They jumped and jostled and jigged about, pulling his ears, hiding his boots and kicking the suitcase that Mother Rabbit was patiently packing. Father Rabbit (who rather fancies himself as a dramatic actor) continued: "I must go, dear Family, to play my part in the GREAT CABBAGE RUSH! Following the stars to the edge of the Great Beyond . . ." (nobody knew where this was so nobody said anything) "I seek good fortune for all of us – a mountain of magnificent CABBAGE SEEDS! We shall be rich and famous and live in a real house. A LARGE house with a real roof and a smokeless chimney!"

This sounded pretty impressive, so a few of the little ones cheered. The older rabbits, like Thumper and Rocky, wanted to join the

Cabbage Rush too, but, as Father Rabbit pointed out, one Hero in a family was quite sufficient. Mother Rabbit said very little, it was Monday morning and she had the washing to see to. Secretly, she considered the Great Cabbage Rush a load of nonsense invented by Uncle Soames . . . and yet, a real house, a really *Large House*, sounded rather splendid . . .

Everybody in PenDelfin Village gathered on the river bank to speed Father Rabbit on the great adventure. It was very touching. Even the crotchety old wedding guest was there. He watched the launching of the home-made raft, he criticised the loading of the barrel of provisions – and he said again, as he said before: "It can't last, of course, it can't last! Whether he meant the raft or the barrel . . . *still* nobody bothered to ask.

The full story of the trials and triumphs of the Great Cabbage Rush may never be told. All Mother Rabbit knows is that one bright morning in Spring, a stately painted barge came sailing up the river. Its deck was piled with presents and its hold was stuffed with CABBAGE SEEDS – the biggest ever seen. FATHER RABBIT WAS HOME!

The Family hardly recognised him ... he was so smart that Mother Rabbit dropped him a shy curtsey and young Rolly whipped out his autograph album. And the *presents* ...

Everybody in PenDelfin Village received a beautiful little gift. A necklace, a watch, an ivory comb, each elegantly wrapped and tied with silver ribbon. They also received (but this was in strict secrecy) a substantial share of the cabbage seed cargo in the hold of the stately barge.

Mother Rabbit and the Family had an exciting time unpacking the treasures for the Hole Homestead. Paintings from Italy, rare tapestries from France, carvings of jade, Chinese carpets of finest silk ... The path of the Great Cabbage Rush must certainly have circled the globe. "My!" said Mother Rabbit, "O My!"

"Send for Boswell!" cried Father Rabbit, "The time has come at last for the building of THE HOUSE!"

This picture is from the Rabbit Family
Album. The main foundation of the House is
a sawn-off tree trunk on the river bank.

All the Family helped with the building –
but some helped more than others . . .

The Building of the House

Boswell is the literary member of the Rabbit Family. He is highly respected in PenDelfin Village, because he can read and write and calculate costs without counting on his paws. Boswell knows exactly 'how many beans make five' – which is important in a place where one cabbage seed is worth a hundred beans . . .

"This new House must be LARGE," he said,

"It certainly must!" said Father Rabbit:

"– and it must be BEAUTIFUL," said Boswell,

"It certainly must!" said Mother Rabbit, (who had already chosen the carpets and most of the furniture . . .)

"Above all," ended Boswell, "it must be HOMELIKE!" Here, all the little rabbits cheered like mad. Especially the untidy ones, like Barney and Dodger, who would much rather have stayed in the old Hole Homestead where they could spill ink and milk and forget to wipe the mud off their boots.

18

Rolly, who is slightly more sensible, helped Boswell to make lists of everybody's requests and suggestions . . . Some were silly and some were sound; like Mother Rabbit's instructions for her Dream Kitchen:

"It must," she said, "be the largest, brightest, room in the House. It must have a smooth slate floor and a big hot stove – for all the Family to gather round in the winter.

"It must have a genuine old Welsh Dresser, with rows of lovely blue and white plates and sensible drawers for balls of string and sticking plasters, and precious old gardening books – (which I hate to throw away!)

"The walls must be lined with cupboards; with wide shelves for my jams and pickles and rare preserves – and a strongly built compartment for Father Rabbit's wine-making jars, which (as we are all aware) have been known to explode in the night! The ceiling must be high. With twisty beams and lots of hooks for strings of onions and bunches of herbs and wet raincoats and a great ship's bell for Clanger to clang in Time of Trouble . . ."

Here, Mother Rabbit ran out of breath, which is hardly surprising.

Boswell's desk was piled high with more and more 'requests'...

The rest of the Family immediately joined in with many more suggestions, but it was Victoria who had the brightest idea of all.

Little, loving, rather bossy Victoria, who takes care of the babies (and sometimes wallops one) – washes the dishes (and sometimes drops one) – and who shares so many of Mother Rabbit's hopes and plans. It was Victoria who thought of building the new House close to the old Hole Homestead, so that the Family would still have their lovely old herb-scented garden and the view across the river to the misty slopes of Pendle Hill.

Rolly wrote everything down, and Boswell drew the plans. Then, with great ceremony (and a rather boring speech) Father Rabbit cut the first turf – and the building began.

It was a Family affair. Everybody joined in, even the artful Dodger, who usually makes himself scarce. Digging and ditching, hammering and sawing, measuring and arguing, as real home-handymen do. Even the babies, like Snuggles and Poppet, were allowed to stay up and help; cutting their teeth on the tough oak pegs that Father Rabbit was carving for the roof tiles.

And all the time, as the House grew larger and more splendid, the Family grew more inventive . . . Boswell's desk was piled high with more and more 'requests' . . .

Thumper needed a Music Room for the Honky-tonk piano. Rocky and Rolly wanted a Disco Den with flashing lights and soundproof walls. Victoria politely requested a 'quite small' Ballroom with lots of mirrors for her ballet lessons – and Whopper hoped for a Tropical Indoor Pool, with 'just a few' leaping dolphins. Midge and Oliver (always hungry) put their names down for 'Personal and Private' Ice-cream Parlours, for small rabbits with large appetites.

Boswell threw down his pen in despair.

"This," he said, "is just hopeless, we shall

never fit everything in!"

He thought of the deep, spacious rooms in the old Homestead, so lovingly hollowed out over the years and soon to be deserted. He thought of the wide sandy passages, each with its own secret door, leading out to different parts of the Pendle countryside. Then, suddenly, he realised that one such passage ran directly underneath Mother Rabbit's new kitchen . . .

Late that night, whilst the rest of the Family slept, three twinkling lanterns appeared on the river bank. With giggles and whispers and a clinking of spade on pebble, Boswell, Whopper and Rocky, tiptoed back to the Large House. It was almost finished. Just one thing remained to be done before the Grand Opening. In a corner of the vast Dream Kitchen, quickly, neatly, and as quietly as possible, they began to dig.

This is how the Large House came to have a fine, sweeping staircase in its kitchen, leading down to a magical mixture of rooms, and passages leading to unexpected places . . .

This is the evening of the Grand Opening of the Large House. Mother and Father Rabbit are the Guests of Honour. The Family had planned a quiet little house-warming party – but everybody in the Village turned up. They are all inside the House – waiting for the corks to pop . . .

The last word about the new House came from Uncle Soames (on a flying visit from the States). Proudly, Father Rabbit had given him a conducted tour. Beginning with the fur-lined Nursery at the top of the House, where all the babies in bed wriggled and bubbled and pretended to be asleep; down through the Pink room, the Green room, the blue and silver Drawing room – right through Mother Rabbit's splendid Kitchen and down the final stairway to the old Hole Homestead . . . "My giddy Aunt!" puffed Soames. At *last* he was impressed.

The dear old Hole had been transformed into a perfect cavern of delights. A Music Room, a Disco Den, a lovely little Ballroom, and a deep green Tropical Pool with two rubber dolphins. The Ice-cream Parlours had not been taken seriously; instead, the Family had built a Games room, a Bowling Alley and a cosy Do-it-yourself Cinema for Father Rabbit's home movies.

"Now that's what I call *Smart,* little brother," said Uncle Soames, shaking him warmly by the paw, "– that's what I call *real* SMART!"

Picnic Island

Excitement in the Large House took quite a time to settle down. After all the fun of building (slurping about with buckets of wet cement and slapping on the whitewash) and all the thrilling business of moving in – with everything new and shining, the Rabbit Family gradually discovered that there is more to life than having every wish granted.

Nobody said anything, just at first, but then the niggles began . . .

Mother Rabbit loved her Dream Kitchen; but she found it just a little bit draughty, and the big new stove (which the Family certainly *did* gather round) just a little bit smoky and difficult to light . . . in fact Father Rabbit was kept pretty busy chopping logs to keep it going.

Victoria was delighted with her Ballroom, but as it was in the basement, and most of Victoria's time was spent upstairs in the Nursery, she found it simpler to dance up there with the little ones – as she always had done.

As for Whopper, although he was pleased with his Tropical Pool, he hated the leaping dolphins. "Rubber!" he grumbled, "Flippin' rubber fish!" – as a true fisherman he felt deeply insulted. One dark night, he carried them outside and tossed them into the river. Sweet Pendle Water carried them into the River Calder – and the Calder carried them out to sea. They were never seen again . . .

Boswell was pretty mad when he heard about it, having taken a great deal of trouble trying to please everyone . . .

"Nothing is ever enough!" he sniffed, "The more some people get, the more some people want . . ." which was hardly fair, because all that the Family really wanted was the old quiet life on the river bank and a little less cabbage-seed High Living.

"What this Family needs," said Mother Rabbit, "is a PICNIC . . . Send for Rosa!"

Rosa's picnics are famous. Everything possible is packed. From cricket bats to jelly spoons, from corkscrews for Father Rabbit's cowslip wine to safety pins for the babies' bibs. (Just once or twice she has been known to forget to pack the food!)

Rosa is a career girl, a very independent young rabbit. She lives in Cobble Cottage, just across the river from the Large House. She paints, and sews, and plays several musical instruments including the tambourine. She also bakes delicious cakes (some to eat and some to sell) – and no Rabbit Family outing would be complete without her.

She was delighted when Whopper arrived in his rowing boat to invite her to the picnic. In a twinkling, out came her basket – and in went a marzipan cake stuffed with nuts and cherries, a rich chocolate log and a very large, very juicy, strawberry tart – (just as Whopper had hoped!) – then away they splashed to the jetty, where Father Rabbit was already packing the Family into the stately barge.

All morning, Mother Rabbit and Victoria had been baking pies, tossing crisp green salads and cutting mounds of tasty assorted sandwiches. All the babies had been scrubbed and combed and stuffed into unsinkable life-jackets. All, except Snuggles – who sleeps through most things – so could hardly be expected to fall into trouble.

(Unlike *some* members of the Family . . .)

At last, with everybody and everything securely stowed on board, Father Rabbit took the helm, Clanger sat with his bell in the prow, and the stately barge, freshly painted and gay with coloured flags, went chugging down the river.

The weather was perfect. The water danced and shimmered in the sunlight, the riverbank glowed with buttercup gold; and the rare, slow, peace of the Village unfolded as they floated by.

They passed the Tavern, where Uncle Soames had stayed, they passed the old broken-down bandstand and the Village Green, where a few stray ribbons still fluttered from the Maypole – and on past the old Curiosity Shop where Boswell lives alone. (He sometimes has to escape from the Family, to his books and his writing and his own private dreams.)

Presently, just ahead, beyond the cool green shadows of the Bluebell Wood, they could see the sunlit beach of Picnic Island.

"Land ahoy!" cried Clanger, swinging his bell . . . "Land ahoy!" yelled everybody else, and the barge ground gently ashore . . .

Whopper and Rolly on the beach.

It was the perfect place for a picnic; sandy shallows to paddle in and deep, clear pools for diving. At some time, long ago, some kindly person had built a great stone fireplace, and left pans and kettles and toasting forks close by in a hollow tree.

Everyone in the Village loved it – and each time they came, found something new; a cave, a rope bridge, a tree-swing – or simply an old golf ball to kick about.

"Now," said Father Rabbit, when everyone and everything was safely ashore, "EVERYBODY SCATTER! We need wood for the fire – lots of dry twigs."

Away hopped the Family in all directions and back they came with kindling for a year. Soon, the fire was crackling and the kettle was singing; the time had come (because they were all very hungry) for the long awaited opening of the picnic baskets . . .

This is when the trouble began.

"Where," said Mother Rabbit, "is the marzipan cake?"

"Where," said Rosa, "is the strawberry tart?"

"Where," said Whopper, "is that dodgy little DODGER – and that greedy little rabbit called MIDGE?"

Where indeed?

Where is the
Strawberry tart?

All the Family know that Dodger hates picnics. He hates the sand, which always gets into *his* sandwich, he hates the wasps, which always seem to settle on *his* cream bun, and, above all, he hates the WORK.

All the running about, collecting firewood, all the filling of kettles and scouring of pans, there is only one good thing about a picnic (thinks Dodger) and that is a well filled picnic basket.

Very quietly and without fuss, whilst the others bustled about, chopping wood and building windbreaks and nipping their paws in difficult deck-chairs, the very artful Dodger had sneaked himself – and his cushion – and a fair-sized picnic basket (Rosa's) – into the cool, shady, shelter of a thorn bush. Here, he settled down to a selfish, work-free feast.

As he opened the basket a most mouth-watering fragrance arose – of apples and almonds and rich crispy pastry; he was just about to sink his teeth into a huge strawberry tart when somebody sniffed, loudly and greedily, over his shoulder . . .

"Hello, DODGER!" yelled Midge in his ear, "Having a nice private PICNIC, are we?" –

and snatching up the tart, off he hopped for a private little picnic of his own. Dodger was furious.

"Just you wait! – you greedy little cotton-tail," he called, "– just wait and see what happens to fat little thieving rabbits. Remember what Victoria tells the babies: 'BEWARE OF THE BIG BAD BOY-O!'"

When Midge heard this he laughed so much that he almost choked on a strawberry. Everybody in PenDelfin Village had heard of the Boy-o, but few had ever seen it. Even Father Rabbit (who had seen most things in his travels around the world) was inclined to believe that the Boy-o was a bogey-man invented by Victoria to make the baby rabbits behave themselves.

"Who's afraid of the Big Bad Boy-o!" sang Midge – and off he danced, sticky with tart, to see if Mother Rabbit had unpacked the turnip pies . . .

With a sigh of relief, Dodger watched him go. Then, after polishing off a couple of apples and a slice or two of cake, he buried his nose in his cushion and went comfortably to sleep.

Whilst Dodger slept and Midge stuffed himself, Victoria was being her own busy little self . . .

Victoria *loves* picnics. Especially on Picnic Island. She loves the sail down the river and the busy bustle of landing and unpacking and helping to build a tent of leaves (in case it rains). She enjoys showing the babies how to make beautiful things – like daisy-chains and cowslip-balls, and (most important) how to tell a mushroom from a toadstool.

Sometimes, her good friend, Casanova, comes across the stepping stones from his caravan in the Bluebell Wood, to teach the older rabbits Romany lore.

The Dodger . . .

On this particular day, Victoria had chosen a
sheltered honeysuckle-scented hollow for the
babies. They were hot and over-tired and
inclined to be naughty.

One of the twins had been stung by a bee –
and the other had come up in a sympathetic
bump. They had both been dabbed with
Tincture-of-Bluebag and rocked to sleep in the
safety of the stately barge.

Once more, all was peace on the Island.

Mother Rabbit nodded and knitted in her deck-chair, Rosa was quietly sketching, Father Rabbit and the boys were playing cricket on the beach and Victoria felt very much 'in charge'. As she tucked up the little ones for their afternoon nap, Rosa heard her say, in a Mother Rabbit sort of voice:

"Here's a kiss for Parsley, *eat your biscuit nicely, dear, and don't make crumbs in the bed* . . .

"Here's a kiss for Wakey – *and put that ladybird back in its box or I'll box your little fat ears!*

"Here's a kiss for Peeps – *and both eyes closed, if you please, my lad – or the Big Bad Boy-o will get you!*

"Here's a kiss for pretty little Poppet, who is already fast asleep. And here is a great big kiss for . . . *SNUGGLES!*"

Her scream brought everyone running.

Snuggles was gone! The treasure of the Family (with pillow, sleeping-bag and half a soggy biscuit) had completely vanished. All that remained was the other half of the biscuit – and a little red cotton sock . . .

"My baby!" shrieked Mother Rabbit, "My

darling child has been stolen! Send for the Fire Brigade! Notify Interpol! Inform Her Majesty the Queen!"

To and fro she trotted, wringing her paws and mopping her eyes – with Barney bawling loudly at her heels and the other little rabbits (who thought it was a fine new game) tumbling in and out of her footprints in the sand.

Mainly because of this, it was some time before Father Rabbit and the more sensible members of the Family found the faint trail of biscuit crumbs leading down to the water's edge . . . and the pawprints of a very large animal.

●　　●　　●　　●

Dodger was still in his hiding place in the thorn bush, his nose comfortably buried in his cushion. He was dreaming of bells ... jingle bells, church bells, ship's bells, alarm bells – CLANGER'S BELL!

"Bother!" said Dodger, warily opening one eye, "something must be wrong –" and "Crumbs!" he said, widely opening the other – "it certainly is!" For sharing his bush, half hidden in the shadows, was a huge striped creature with glowing amber eyes . . . and nestling between its paws, fast asleep, without a care in the world, was Snuggles!

Now, Dodger has never pretended to be a hero, he much prefers comfort to glory, finding himself nose to nose with trouble he decided to 'mind his manners'.

"Good afternoon – Sir!" he said.

The creature growled, in a hungry sort of way. The amber eyes narrowed. The fierce striped head bowed low – and a pink tongue gave Snuggles a thoughtful lick. Dodger was alarmed. "I suppose, S-Sir," he stammered, "that you wouldn't care for a piece of c-cake . . . instead?"

"CAKE?" roared the creature, "CAKE? *I eat little rabbits for breakfast!* How *dare* you offer cake to the BOY-O?"

This is when Dodger's courage failed him. With a mighty leap, he left his cushion and buried his nose in the river. Away he splashed, bubbling with fright, to tell Father Rabbit all about it.

The whole Island rang with Dodger's news: "Snuggles has been captured by the BIG BAD BOY-O!"

His courage failed him . . .

It completely ruined the picnic.

Mother Rabbit fainted right away and had to be revived with a stiff dose of prune juice. Father Rabbit armed himself with a cudgel and lined up the Family for action.

"Search every inch of the Island," he commanded, "Give no quarter, fight to the death!" Barney cheered and waved his hatchet, then burst into tears because Victoria bustled him into the safety of the barge with the other babies.

Oddly enough, Victoria was the calmest and coolest member of the Family.

(But then, *she* knows Snuggles . . .)

Round and round the Island they went, following the great pawprints; until they were completely covered by everybody else's pawprints. They searched the beach, they combed the caves, they climbed the trees and called: "Snuggles! – SNU-GG-GLES . . ." but the only trace of him to be found was the other little red cotton sock.

Suddenly, Whopper called a halt.

"Listen!" he said, his sharp ears twitching under his sou'wester, "There it goes again!"

This time everyone heard it. A high, shrill

scream . . .

"My child!" cried Mother Rabbit, "It is the voice of my little one!" – and she promptly fainted again.

"Nonsense!" said Victoria, "it sounds more like a cat being bitten by a mouse!"

Soon it would be dark, already a thin mist was rising from the river, and Father Rabbit realised that the Island could be a very dangerous place for young rabbits at night. He felt it wise to call off the search until the following day. Poor Mother Rabbit was tenderly placed in the stately barge (having been given another dose of prune juice) – and away went the Family, with very heavy hearts.

(The reason that nobody thought of looking in the thorn bush was that Dodger, in his fright, had completely forgotten where it was!)

As the plaintive foghorn of the barge echoed sadly across the water, Snuggles sat up and sneezed. He had been wide awake for quite some time, ever since Dodger dived into the river; now he was hungry.

Usually, the moment Snuggles woke up somebody gave him a little bite of something tasty; a turnip top – or a lump of sugar – or even a dandelion lollipop. The only thing that he had found to sink his sharp little teeth into had been the ear of the Big Bad Boy-o.

It had been a mistake and Snuggles was sorry. But (he thought) if some people *will* go a-dangling their great furry heads over other people's teeth – then *some* people are going to get nipped.

And a fine screeching they made!

. . . even Boswell, away across the river in the old Curiosity Shop, must have heard it – but, of course, he was busy writing his memoirs and would be thinking of other things . . .

Snuggles frowned at the Boy-o and the Boy-o frowned back. It was feeling foolish. It had never been bitten by a rabbit before, especially a *baby* rabbit curled up in a sleeping-bag – like a plump and delicious sausage roll.

Boswell heard it!

"Once bitten is a bite too many!" it growled, "now it is *my* turn, little fat sausage . . ." and the hungry Boy-o crawled slowly and stealthily nearer . . . and nearer and its quivering nose came closer . . . and closer . . . until suddenly – *SNAP!* – that plump and delicious little sausage had siezed that nose in its sharp little rabbit teeth!

This time, the howling of the Boy-o could be heard all over the Village. Up and down the river bank people sitting down to supper, or being tucked up in bed for the night, shivered and dithered and hoped that somebody braver would go to find out what was wrong.

"Witches and boggarts . . ." grumbled the old and crotchety rabbit, pulling his night cap over his ears, "– they can't last, you know, they can't *last* . . ." and he hid his head under the sheets.

In the old Curiosity Shop, Boswell wiped his pen and put away his papers. Then, with a lantern in one paw and a good stout stick in the other, he went to find out for himself.

Out on the river, the first thing to be seen was the stately barge. Boswell hailed it at once. On board, all was panic.

At the first scream, Mother Rabbit had fainted again – and the whole Family had been dosed with prune juice to restore order. Nobody knew what was happening on the Island – so, naturally, everybody offered advice. Father Rabbit (who was particularly glad to see Boswell and his stout stick) promptly turned the barge about – and back they went, full speed ahead, to the rescue.

Victoria (who knows Snuggles *very well indeed*) sat calmly in the stern, knitting . . .

On Picnic Island, the mist had cleared and the moon had risen. Two figures could be seen, sitting side by side on the beach, a very large stripey one and a very small pinkish one. Nearby, on the sand, lay Rosa's missing picnic basket – empty.

"That," the Boy-o was saying, licking the crumbs from his paws, "was the most delicious marzipan cake that I ever did taste." His companion gave a gentle burp. Snuggles, as usual, was already fast asleep.

Very cautiously, taking great care not to wake him, the Boy-o picked up Snuggles by his sleeping bag and carried him like a kitten to the water's edge. There, on a little piece of tree-bark, rather like a boat, he launched him onto Pendle Water, trusting that gentle river to carry him home. "Thank you for the picnic," called the Boy-o, as he leaped away over the stepping-stones and vanished into the Bluebell Wood, "– and thank you," (here, you could tell that he was holding his nose) – "thank you very butch for the sticking blaster!"

This is how Snuggles came to be found, asleep on the river and covered in crumbs. Of the big Bad Boy-o, the Family saw not a whisker. But rumour has it that on a farm on Pendle Hill lives a great striped cat – who from that day forth – would eat nothing but marzipan cakes.

The Rabbit Band

The Band was Casanova's idea.

Casanova is a Romany friend of the Rabbit Family. He lives in the Bluebell Wood in a splendid caravan and pretends to despise people who live in ordinary houses. The Large House, of course, is not an ordinary house — which is why Casanova spends so much time there.

On the morning of the Great Idea, he was sitting on the steps, idly strumming on his mandolin and watching the ducks sail by —

"Just like a Parade," he said to Rocky, who had joined him on the doorstep, "dipping and bobbing and paddling in step."

"All they need is the music!" said Rocky, twanging his guitar.

Together the two young rabbits played to the ducks. Immediately, from every corner of the Large House, from the tin whistles and toy drums of the babies in the Nursery to the tinkle of the Honky-tonk piano in the basement – the Family joined in.

From the work-shop came the wail of Father Rabbit's musical-saw, from the kitchen came a ripple of bells – and the tuneful clinking of assorted bottles as Oliver whacked them with his wooden spoon.

The whole of the river bank leaped and rocked . . . "A BAND! A BAND! A RABBIT BAND!" cried Casanova . . . and that was decided upon.

Everybody in the village was invited to join. Even the old and crotchety rabbit was persuaded to play the triangle. It was old and rusty (like himself) and had been in his family for many years – "It may not *look* very much," he said to Casanova, "but at least, it *will last!*"

As the news spread, distant relatives in

far-away places sent old and cherished instruments. A drum from Bongo (in the Congo), a trumpet from Phumf (in the Persian Gulf) a battered concertina from Squeezy – and a lovely old song book (in Welsh) from Megan the Harp.

Mother Rabbit was delighted to hear from them all and Father Rabbit seemed truly thankful that they had all settled down happily, elsewhere.

Uncle Soames sent a postcard with all good wishes – and the news that he would soon be home. Everybody hoped that the Rabbit Band would be in reasonably good working order before he arrived – for there was no telling what schemes he might get up to . . .

Choosing a Conductor was quite a problem. The best musicians (mainly Thumper, Rocky and Casanova) chose to play in the Band, whilst Rosa, who had a great many other things to do, was happy just to play the tambourine.

Barney – (who volunteered because he thought that a Band Conductor was pretty much the same as a Bus Conductor) – was turned down flat.

He cried, of course.

The one member of the Family nobody thought of asking was – Whopper.

Whopper is always thought of as a sporting, out-door sort of rabbit, which, of course, he is – but he has fine hidden talents.

Under that floppy sou'wester lies a wide knowledge of a number of things not usually known to rabbits, such as French, and Welsh, and MUSIC.

When Whopper first sat down to play the Honky-tonk piano, everybody laughed. Which was hardly surprising because he is a terrible pianist. But, when he marched up to Father Rabbit and siezed the Conductor's baton and rapped it smartly for attention – everybody leaped to it!

He has proved himself to be an ideal conductor. He knows how to keep order, without hurting people's feelings, and has been able to persuade Rosa not to sing.

The Curiosity Shop did a roaring trade in old sheet music and old fashioned band parts. Boswell had to put away his pen and papers to attend to the tinkle of the shop bell and spent most of his time polishing battered bugles and re-stringing violins.

The first Band Practice was held in the elegant little music room of the Large House.

Mother Rabbit and Victoria worked hard all morning, baking scones and cutting sandwiches and setting out the best china on fine silver trays. As the Grandfather clock in the hall chimed the hour, the first musician arrived; and then the next and the next – until the music room was a heaving, hopping mass of musically-minded rabbits.

Everybody in the village seemed to be there (most of them for Mother Rabbit's scones) – all tightly packed from wall to wall. Fiddlers jabbed sharp elbows into the ribs of trumpeters. Trumpeters blasted loudly into the ears of drummers – and all the drummers, especially the smallest ones, thumped away regardless of the Conductor and deafened everybody for miles around.

As a Band Practice it was a complete disaster – until Whopper took charge. He restored order simply by yelling:

"TEA TIME!"

In two minutes the room was empty – and the Great Hall, where Mother Rabbit sat guarding a giant tea urn, was comfortably

54

full. Everybody ate a lot and drank a lot and laughed a lot, until all tempers were restored to sweetness. Even the temper of the crotchety old rabbit – who had just been about to accuse baby Parsley of cutting her tooth on his triangle.

A happy, giddy time was had by all, but, as Father Rabbit was beginning to realise, there is more to forming a Band than meets the ear!

The second Band Practice was held on the Village Green. This time, the Family tactfully let it be known that neither scones nor sandwiches would be provided – (to say nothing of silver trays). Very few of the Villagers turned up. The crotchety rabbit stumped off home and hung up his triangle with his hat.

"Bands!" he grumbled, "who needs Bands? – I just *knew* that it couldn't last!"

The serious musicians, like Rocky and Casanova, remained – and practised hard. In a very short time they began to sound like a really fine thorough-going Band.

Another picture from the Family Album.

The Honky-tonk piano, being old and very fragile, had to be wheeled with great care to every Band Practice.

The little hand-cart appears by kind permission of Blossom, the owner of the Village Fruit Shop. Barrow-Boy, Blossom's assistant, is not in the picture because he was practising the flute in the Castle Tavern. His favourite tune, according to Boswell, is called 'Wetting the Whistle'.

. . . wheeled with great care . . .

Father Rabbit was so pleased with the Band that he completely rebuilt the broken old bandstand on the Village Green. Not to be outdone, Mother Rabbit and Rosa surrounded it with elegant continental-looking chairs, and tables with brightly striped sunshades.

On the day of the first performance a large tent appeared, bearing the words: TEA TENT. FREE TO ALL-COMERS.

Needless to say, all came.

Back came the Villagers; some to listen and some to play – and this time, scones or no scones – they came to play with a will . . .

As Whopper, standing proudly on the Bandstand, raised his baton for this first Public Performance, a great and wonderful joy filled his heart. The Fiddlers fiddled, the Harpists harped, the Drummers and the Trumpeters rattled and blew and the dear old Honky-tonk piano almost danced itself off its tottery wooden legs.

The first performance was such a success that it was decided to hold regular Band Concerts. Once a month – weather permitting.

The fame of the PenDelfin Village Band spread quickly. Soon, rival Bands from every corner of Pendle Forest sprang up.

Rabbits from Barley, rabbits from Fence, rabbits from Newchurch and from old, enchanting Roughlee – all forming Bands of their own and challenging Father Rabbit's Family.

He was astonished – and delighted.

Every challenge was happily accepted and great and unbelieveable was the excitement and preparation for:

THE GREAT RABBIT BAND CONTEST.

Uncle Soames, who hates to miss anything, speeded up his travelling plans and flew home at once. In his luggage, safely packed in a velvet-lined case, was a magnificent silver shield for the winning Band. A picture of it (and Uncle Soames) appeared in the evening edition of the "Warren Gossip" – to be admired by all.

As the day of the Contest drew near, the excitement grew. It is amazing just how many rabbits, both wild and tame, live around Pendle Hill.

In they poured by cart and caravan, until the tiny Village of PenDelfin was filled to overflowing. Every spare room in every

. . . a fine old time . . .

cottage, every corner of the Castle Tavern –
(except, of course, Uncle Soames' private
suite) – was packed with music and musicians,
talking, playing, hopping and dancing, having
a fine old time.

At the Large House, Mother Rabbit's
kitchen was stacked to its twisty beams with
freshly baked bread and cakes and pies – to
feed this army of competitors; whilst down
below, in the old Hole Homestead, an untold
number made themselves at home on
comfortable camp-beds in Victoria's little
Ballroom. They enjoyed the odd plunge into
Whopper's Tropical Indoor Pool and practised
their band-parts in the Music Room. (They
enjoyed themselves so much that Father
Rabbit had great difficulty in persuading them
to go home after the Contest.)

Late comers, were not quite so fortunate.
They simply pitched their tents by the river
and hoped for fine weather.

At last, the great day dawned.
It was bright and sunny and the Village had
never looked lovelier. Coloured flags flew from
the windows of the houses, garlands of fresh
flowers hung from the trees, as each Band,

from each part of the Forest, paraded along the river-path and round and round the Bandstand on the Village Green.

Here, in a great circle, each village banner fluttering in the breeze, they waited to play – and to be judged.

Now, this business of judging had been rather a problem. All the competitors agreed that Uncle Soames should be asked to present the prizes – (they were wonderfully impressed by the silver shield) – but *nobody* agreed to his judging the Contest. Partly because he was related to the members of a competing Band – but mostly because he cannot tell one end of a flute from the other!

It was finally decided, by Whopper and the other Conductors, that the RABBIT BAND CONTEST would be judged by the good old fashioned rabbit method of a Thumping Round of Applause.

And so it began.

Band after Band, climbing on the Bandstand in search of glory and the glittering silver prize. Some were good, some were very good, just a few were terrible.

The Family stood shoulder to shoulder,

clutching their instruments and awaiting their turn to play. As the afternoon wore on the sun grew hotter and tempers began to boil. Ice-cream was hastily handed round to cool everybody down.

The Barley Band played beautifully, the circle of rabbits round the Bandstand cheered and thumped their little tails on the grass – and *every thump scored a mark* for Barley.

The Band from Fence played better still, (until a barrel-organ was discovered in their midst!). It was when the Band from Roughlee, in splendid crimson uniforms, began to play their strange and haunting music of the Hill, that Whopper's heart sank down to his goloshes ... for the audience sat as though bewitched and as the music ended, they whooped and yelled and thumped each other – *instead of thumping the grass.*

"NO SCORE!" roared the oldest, most crotchety rabbit, who was bossily in charge of the score-board. And home stumped the furious Roughlee Band, each with a small consolation prize and muttering threats of vengeance – (which is quite another story) . . .

At the end of the day, every single musician in every single Band received a splendid bronze medal – and an invitation to a most magnificent supper party at the Large House. Most of the Village came too.

Oh, by the way, the silver shield, as everybody rather expected, was awarded to the PenDelfin Village Band – not because they were the best musicians – but because they all stayed behind and helped to clear up the mess . . .

The End